SILENT BUT DI

'Time for a terrific teacher's tinkle!' sang
Mr Watts to himself as he unzipped his trousers.

A cloud of dirty, green gas rose slowly above
the cubicle door behind him. It floated silently
towards the science teacher.

Suddenly, a zombie's arm shot from it and
a powerful, green hand grabbed Mr Watts by
the throat. The teacher stared in horror at the
creature that was now lifting him a metre off
the ground. Flakes of olive skin peeled away
from the zombie's face and piercing red eyes
stared down at him.

'No! Please!' screamed Mr Watts, as the
monster rose above him, yellowing teeth bared.
Green saliva dripped from a thick, green tongue.

The science teacher screwed his eyes shut as
the zombie roared and pounced upon its prey.

St Sebastian's School in Grimesford is the pits. No, really — it is.

Every year, the high school sinks a bit further into the boggy plague pit beneath it and, every year, the ghosts of the plague victims buried underneath it become a bit more cranky.

Egged on by their spooky ringleader, Edith Codd, they decide to get their own back — and they're willing to play dirty. *Really* dirty.

They kick up a stink by causing as much mischief as in inhumanly possible so as to get St Sebastian's closed down once and for all.

But what they haven't reckoned on is year-seven new boy, James Simpson and his friends Alexander and Lenny.

The question is, are the gang up to the challenge of laying St Sebastian's paranormal problem to rest, or will their school remain forever frightful?

There's only one way to find out . . .

www.too-ghoul.com

TOO GHOUL FOR SCHOOL

Silent But Deadly

B. STRANGE

EGMONT

Special thanks to:

Tommy Donbavand, St John's Walworth Church of England Primary School and Belmont Primary School

EGMONT
We bring stories to life

Published in Great Britain 2007
by Egmont UK Limited
239 Kensington High Street, London W8 6SA

Text and Illustrations © 2007 Egmont UK Ltd
Text by Tommy Donbavand
Illustrations by Pulsar Studio (Beehive Illustration)

ISBN 978 1 4052 3235 7

1 3 5 7 9 10 8 6 4 2

A CIP catalogue record for this title is available
from the British Library

Typeset by Avon DataSet Ltd, Bidford on Avon, Warwickshire
Printed and bound in Great Britain by the CPI Group

'More books – I love it!'
Ashley, age 11

'It's disgusting. . .'
Joe, age 10

'. . . it's all good!'
Alexander, age 9

'. . . loads of excitement and really gross!'
Jay, age 9

'I like the way there's the brainy boy,
the brawny boy and the cool boy that form a
team of friends'
Charlie, age 10

'That ghost Edith is wicked'
Matthew, age 11

'This is really good and funny!'
Sam, age 9

We want to hear what *you* think about
Too Ghoul for School! Visit:

www.too-ghoul.com

for loads of cool stuff to do
and a whole lotta grot!

School versus...

Year-seven new boy
and chief spook-hunter

James Simpson

Headmaster's son
and official brainiac

Alexander Tick

Strong as an ox,
gentle as an
unusually tall lamb

Lenny Maxwell

... Ghoul!

Loud-mouthed
ringleader of the
plague-pit ghosts

Edith Codd

Young ghost and
a secret wannabe
St Sebastian's pupil

William Scroggins

Bone idle ex-leech
merchant with a taste
for all things gross

Ambrose Harbottle

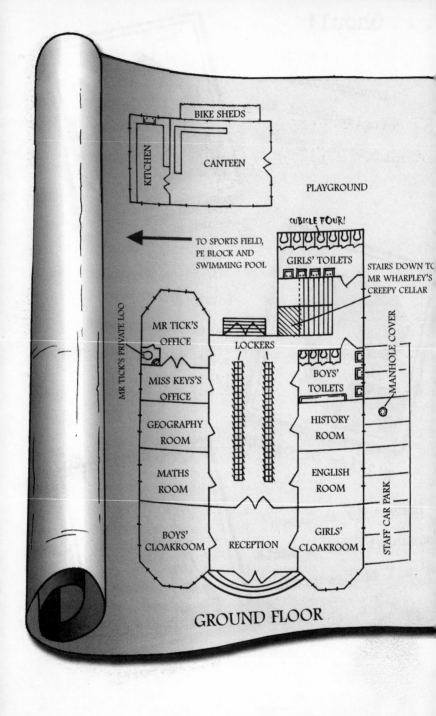

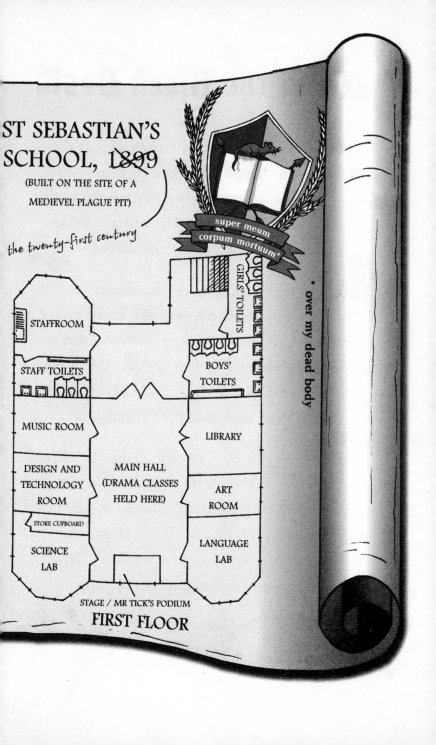

ST SEBASTIAN'S SCHOOL, ~~1899~~

(BUILT ON THE SITE OF A
MEDIEVEL PLAGUE PIT)

the twenty-first century

**super meum
corpum mortuum** *

* over my dead body

STAFFROOM

STAFF TOILETS

MUSIC ROOM

DESIGN AND
TECHNOLOGY
ROOM

STORE CUPBOARD

SCIENCE
LAB

MAIN HALL
(DRAMA CLASSES
HELD HERE)

STAGE / MR TICK'S PODIUM

GIRLS' TOILETS

BOYS'
TOILETS

LIBRARY

ART
ROOM

LANGUAGE
LAB

FIRST FLOOR

About the Black Death

The Black Death was a terrible plague that is believed to have been spread by fleas on rats. It swept through Europe in the fourteenth century, arriving in England in 1348, where it killed over one third of the population.

One of the Black Death's main symptoms was **foul-smelling boils all over the body called 'buboes'**. The plague was so infectious that its victims and their families were locked in their houses until they died. Many villages were abandoned as the disease wiped out their populations.

So many people died that graveyards overflowed and bodies lay in the street, so special **'plague pits'** were dug to bury the bodies. Almost every town and village in England has a plague pit somewhere underneath it, so watch out when you're digging in the garden . . .

Dear Reader

As you may have already guessed, B. Strange is not a real name.

The author of this series is an ex-teacher who is currently employed by a little-known body called the Organisation For Spook Termination (Excluding Demons), or O.F.S.T.(E.D.). 'B. Strange' is the pen name chosen to protect his identity.

Together, we felt it was our duty to publish these books, in an attempt to save innocent lives. The stories are based on the author's experiences as an O.F.S.T.(E.D.) inspector in various schools over the past two decades.

Please read them carefully - you may regret it if you don't . . .

Yours sincerely
The Publisher.

PS - Should you wish to file a report on any suspicious supernatural occurrences at your school, visit **www.too-ghoul.com** and fill out the relevant form. We'll pass it on to O.F.S.T.(E.D.) for you.

PPS - All characters' names have been changed to protect the identity of the individuals. Any similarity to actual persons, living or undead, is purely coincidental.

CONTENTS

1   IT'S A GAS   1

2   ALL CHANGE   11

3   CLASS ACT   23

4   CURIOUSER AND CURIOUSER   32

5   PIT OF DESPAIR   41

6   THE PLAN   51

7   HOT AND SPICY   60

8   LOVE HURTS   68

9   GREY MATTER   80

10 SEARCH AND DESTROY   90

11 WE DIG, DIG, DIG . . .   100

12 DOWN AND OUT   110

13 IT MUST BE LOVE   119

    EXTRA! FACT FILE, JOKES AND YUCKY STUFF   131

    THE IN-SPECTRES CALL SNEAK PREVIEW   137

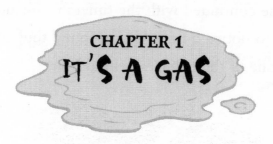

CHAPTER 1
IT'S A GAS

'Time for a terrific teacher's tinkle!' sang
Mr Watts to himself as he unzipped his trousers.
School would be starting in a little under fifteen
minutes' time and a pre-pupil pee was part of his
regular morning routine. It was a chance to run
through the day's schedule without interruptions.

'Double science with year seven to begin with,'
he said aloud, his voice echoing around the
empty staff toilets. 'Followed by break and a cup
of hot tea: two sugars, a splash of milk and a
bourbon biscuit.' Mr Watts was nothing if not

thorough. Science and precise measurements were his life.

As he continued with the timetable ahead, he failed to notice a faint hissing sound that came from one of the cubicles behind him.

Slowly, a cloud of dirty, green gas rose above the cubicle door and turned, seeming to look around the room. It spotted Mr Watts – now busy listing his lunch menu – and floated silently towards him.

'Four potatoes, microwaved for four point five minutes and smothered with approximately four point two five milligrams of butter, two thousand, three hundred grains of salt and a light sprinkling of pepper . . .'

The cloud hovered just centimetres behind Mr Watts's head as he paused to zip up his flies. Moving to the sink, he turned his scientific mind towards his choice of lunchtime meat.

'Roast beef, three slices, each two point five millimetres thick . . .' he began, as he strolled across the bathroom to the soap dispenser. The green cloud kept pace, just out of Mr Watts's vision as he spun the hot tap, pumped liquid soap on to his palms and began to wash.

The cloud braced itself, ready to pounce as soon as Mr Watts had finished rinsing his hands. Ready to overwhelm him – any minute now. Aaaaaany minute . . . now. What was taking this idiot so long? He was only washing his hands, not preparing for surgery!

The cloud sighed and took a moment to glance around the room. Catching sight of itself in the mirror, it floated over and examined what it saw.

Hmmm. A big, floating cloud, thought the big, floating cloud. *Not exactly the scariest shape ever. How terrifying would the science teacher find that? If he ever finished washing his hands and turned around, that was. Plus, cloud shapes were so last year. Definitely time for a change.*

Concentrating hard, the cloud began to rearrange its atoms, searching its limited memory banks for a form that would scare an obsessively clean science teacher. New shape achieved, the cloud turned once again to the mirror to study the horrifying creature it had now become.

A chicken. The cloud had morphed into a chicken.

What was it going to do as a chicken? Peck Mr Watts's calculator to pieces? Shaking its beak, the cloud tried again. Molecules exploded and reformed as the green gas changed shape once more. Ah, this felt better – arms, legs, a weapon in one hand! Let's take a look.

A court jester. A jolly court jester, complete with a stick of jingly bells. The cloud sighed again. Although it was an improvement on the chicken, there must be something scarier it could transform itself into. Perhaps if it searched a mind other than its own . . .

Relaxing, the cloud let its mind drift outside the staff toilets and in to the school beyond. If it could tap in to the consciousness of one or more of the pupils, it could scan their thoughts and take the shape of something that frightened them. Aha! There was a group of year-eight girls. Now to discover their darkest fears . . .

'Three carrots, pre-sliced, swimming in lukewarm water,' continued Mr Watts, still unaware of the mysterious green shape that hovered behind him.

The cloud's shape changed quickly as it leapt unnoticed from mind to mind, seeking out the nightmare visions lurking deep inside the girls' brains.

'One slice of bread with a thin smear of margarine . . .'

A vampire. A swamp monster. A fountain pen. *A fountain pen*? Who's scared of a fountain pen? Ah – here's something. Oh, yes, this one's good. This one's *very* good.

The cloud changed shape for a final time and smiled as Mr Watts dried his hands on a paper towel, whistling merrily.

'And that's lunch sorted!' Tossing the paper towel into the bin, Mr Watts leant in to the mirror to check his thin, chinstrap beard. As he ran his fingers lovingly over the wiry hair, he became aware of a figure standing at the next mirror along.

'Morning, Bob,' Mr Watts grinned at Mr Hall, the history teacher, while checking his nostrils for bogeys. 'How's the industrial revolution treating you?' The figure growled wetly and the smile on Mr Watts's face died as he realised that the person standing beside him wasn't St Sebastian's history teacher after all.

The zombie's arm shot forwards and a powerful, green hand grabbed Mr Watts by the throat. The science teacher stared in horror at the creature that was now lifting him a metre off the ground. Flakes of olive skin peeled away from the zombie's face and piercing red eyes stared down at him.

Mr Watts tried to speak, to plead for his life, but the zombie's grip on his throat was too tight and he could only manage a weak gargling sound. The zombie pulled the teacher forwards, until its nose was touching his. Its vile breath made Mr Watts's eyes water.

'Ggggurrh!' groaned the teacher, struggling to concentrate as blackness came ever closer.

I have to escape, he thought as a wave of unconsciousness began to sweep over him. *I must find a way to beat this ogre. But I know nothing about fighting monsters – I only know science. Perhaps I could use science . . .*

Biology? No – the creature's certainly not human, so I can't use biology against it. Chemistry? What is the monster made of? I don't know, so chemistry's no use. That just leaves physics. Physics!

As his last strands of consciousness began to slip away, Mr Watts swung his leg out at just the right velocity and felt, with satisfaction, his foot connect hard with the contents of the zombie's trousers.

The creature staggered backwards briefly before steadying itself and grabbing the teacher's tie. Swinging him round, the zombie sent him crashing to the floor.

Breathing hard, Mr Watts scrambled to his feet, massaging the bruises that were beginning to appear around his neck. He dashed for the door.

He only managed to turn the handle and open the door a crack before the zombie grabbed his ankle and dragged him back across the slippery floor of the toilets.

'No! Please!' screamed Mr Watts, as the monster rose above him, yellowing teeth bared. Green saliva dripped from a thick, green tongue.

The science teacher screwed his eyes shut as the zombie roared and pounced upon its prey.

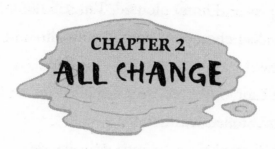

CHAPTER 2
ALL CHANGE

'Fourteen, fifteen, sixteen . . .' Lenny Maxwell counted aloud as his friend James Simpson kept a football in the air with his forehead as they walked to school.

'There's Stacey Carmichael!' blurted Lenny, causing James to spin round, the ball bouncing off his face and into the gutter.

'Where?' asked James, rubbing his nose. Lenny was doubled over with laughter. 'That's not fair!' James protested when he realised Stacey was nowhere to be seen.

'Rule number four of keepie-uppie: players can distract their opponents with verbal insults at any time!' Lenny gloated. 'I'm still the undefeated champion with twenty-three headers in a row!'

'But that wasn't an insult!' replied James. 'You told me Stacey was here!'

Lenny grinned as he retrieved the ball from the roadside. 'Worked though, didn't it?'

'This is turning into a bad morning,' moaned James. '*And* we've got double science first thing!'

'What do you reckon Mr Watts is doing right now?' asked Lenny.

James shrugged. 'Whatever it is, it can't be worse than losing to you at keepie-uppie!'

As the zombie leapt towards him, Mr Watts brought his legs up and managed to push the creature away with his feet. It crashed back against the sinks, but quickly turned, advancing on him again.

Mr Watts jumped up and dashed into one of the cubicles, where he locked the door, vainly hoping that a cheap bolt would somehow hold back a furious, howling beast.

The creature burst into the compartment on its third attempt and grabbed hold of the science teacher's leg as he tried to climb over into the next cubicle. Somehow, Mr Watts fell on top of the zombie and ended up wedged on the raging monster's shoulders.

The zombie staggered backwards, Mr Watts now riding him like a disgusting rodeo stallion. The creature lashed about with its hands, trying to unseat the teacher but, just as he was about to fall, Mr Watts grabbed hold of the light fitting and pulled himself away.

Clinging to a short length of electrical cord, the teacher swung his legs up towards the ceiling and

out of reach of the zombie, who was now leaping
up and down. It growled and snarled and swatted
at Mr Watts like an unwelcome insect.

'I can get you food!' the teacher shouted as the monster continued to rage below him. 'I'm having roast beef for lunch! Would you like some of that? Th-three slices, each a thickness of two point five millimetres?'

As though the thought of such pathetically thin slices of beef angered it even further, the zombie roared and then began to climb on to one of the toilets, giving it the extra height it needed to reach the terrified scientist.

The light fitting finally gave way under the strain and Mr Watts crashed down to the floor, trembling with fear.

The zombie glared down at him from the toilet seat, its eyes flashing. It smiled for a moment, then leapt upon Mr Watts with a roar.

Mr Watts stumbled along the corridor, desperately trying to remember what had just happened to him. He knew he'd visited the staff toilets for his early-morning pee, but everything after that was just a blur. A sort of green blur.

Becoming aware of a throbbing sensation in his neck, he stopped shuffling along the corridor and reached up gingerly to explore the area above the collar of his favourite shirt. He traced

the outline of what felt like teeth marks with his fingers. He shook his head – it couldn't be. Continuing to explore he touched something wet and drew his hand away to inspect it. It was blood.

Still, it'll wash out, he thought to himself. *That's the beauty of shirts made from polyest– polyest–* What was the word? His brain began to hurt as he ran through the possibilities. Polythene? Polystyrene? Polly put the kettle on?

Mr Watts shook his head to try and clear it. Something wasn't right. He felt as though his brain was filled with mud, and his thoughts were having to wade through the gunk to get anywhere.

'Concentrate!' he told himself aloud. 'How can you teach science if you're having to think yourself out of a swamp? Science! That's it. Focus on science and the familiarity will soon bring you to your senses.'

Mr Watts pictured the periodic table of elements before him, something he would normally save for an evening alone in his flat with a can of beer and a pepperoni pizza, but this was an emergency.

OK . . . Hydrogen. Helium. So far, so good. What's next? Lithi–, er, lithi– Lithium! Yes, that's it! Lithium! Mr Watts sighed heavily. Thinking was hard work. Maybe a little exercise would clear the cobwebs.

A group of year-eight boys watched in amazement as their science teacher dropped his briefcase to the floor and attempted to touch his toes, grunting as he stretched his fingertips down towards his sensible shoes.

'Just . . . a little . . . further . . .' muttered Mr Watts, as his hands shook with the effort. But it was no use, and the boys were laughing and pointing at him now. 'They're getting deten–, er . . . deten– Sent to a room were they must sit and work after school,' he told himself. 'Just as soon as I stand up.'

Except he couldn't stand up. Mr Watts groaned as he realised that his spine would no longer straighten out, leaving him with a caveman-like hunch. Moaning in discomfort, the teacher shuffled round to face the group of now hysterical pupils to ask for help.

'I think I've got a slipped disc!' he called. But when the words came out of his mouth, they sounded more like: 'Geh oo urse sip diss!' The gang of boys paused to let this string of nonsense sink in, then burst out laughing again.

Mr Watts grabbed his briefcase and turned away from the group, stumbling down the corridor. *What's happening to me?* he thought. *Why can't I stand up straight, or even talk properly?* He stumbled on. 'Well, whatever the problem is, panicking will only make it worse,' he told himself, firmly. 'Now – breathe slowly, Keith.

In, aaand out. In, aaand out. Slow that heartbeat right down . . .'

THUD . . .

THUD . . .

THUD . . .

Soon, to his horror, the science teacher realised that his heart couldn't beat any slower if it tied itself to an elderly tortoise with a wooden leg.

''elp meee!' he groaned, as he struggled to place one foot in front of the other and reach his classroom. But the pupils streaming past him were too busy laughing to come to his aid.

Perhaps if he wrote it down, someone would help. As he turned the corner towards the science lab, Mr Watts reached into his pocket and pulled out a pen.

By the time he reached the lab, Mr Watts's beard and chin were stained with blue ink. His teeth crunched on what remained of the plastic pen barrel and he swallowed noisily and let out a satisfied sigh.

'Teach! Teach! Teach!' he groaned as he bounced off a doorframe and stumbled into the science storeroom, where he was showered with test tubes and Bunsen burners.

Reappearing, he reached up and scratched his face while deciding which direction to stagger off in. Giant flakes of skin peeled from his cheeks and drifted down to decorate his navy blue tank top.

Raising his fingers up in front of his eyes, he stared numbly at the clump of ink-coloured beard that he clutched in his hand. 'Bleh!' he moaned, tossing the hair aside and lurching back out into the corridor.

A year-eight girl stopped in her tracks and watched, open-mouthed, as Mr Watts tottered unsteadily towards her.

'Is, er . . . everything OK, sir?' she asked.

'Room!' he replied in a deep voice.

'Excuse me, sir?' said the girl, shuddering at the sight of the bits of skin that covered the teacher's clothing.

Mr Watts moaned. 'Roooooom!' he repeated.

The girl glanced around, uncertainly. 'Er, your classroom is the third door on the right, sir,' she said, pressing her back against the wall as the teacher stumbled off in the direction she was pointing.

She stared as Mr Watts dragged himself away, groaning 'Teach! Teach! Teach!' Then, mentally crossing 'science teacher' from her list of possible future careers, she ran away as fast as she could.

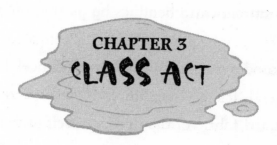

CHAPTER 3
CLASS ACT

'Me and science, sitting in a tree, K-I-S-S-I-N-G!' sang Alexander Tick, happily, as he unpacked textbooks from his school bag and danced a merry little jig around the desk at the same time. James kicked him hard in the shin.

'*Ow!* What did you do that for?' demanded Alexander as he rubbed his bruised leg.

'Everybody's watching you!' hissed James as he glanced up at the sea of giggling faces that filled the classroom behind them.

'*So?*' asked Alexander.

James sighed. 'Doesn't being the headmaster's son make you enough of a target?' he enquired. 'Don't attract extra beatings by putting on a show!'

Alexander shrugged. 'But I love science!' he explained. 'It's the foundation of life on this planet, the fabric of the universe itself and – best of all – my favourite subject for homework!'

'Well, I bet we end up with loads of it today,' moaned James. 'You saw the mood Mr Watts was in yesterday. He had an expression on his face like a bulldog licking vinegar off a thistle!'

'What's this bulldog been doing?' asked Lenny as he strode over the desk and perched his tall frame on the edge of it.

'Drinking vinegar, apparently,' answered Alexander, carefully arranging the pencils on his desk into order of lead hardness.

'It won't be long before it throws up, then,' said Lenny. 'It'll need taking to the vet. Where is it?'

Alexander shrugged. 'I dunno. James was talking about it.'

Lenny turned to the other boy. 'You didn't tell me your mum had got you a dog,' he said.

'She hasn't got me a dog!' exclaimed James, exasperated.

'Oh, found it, did you?' said Lenny. 'Poor thing was probably kicked out of home for puking everywhere if it's been drinking vinegar.'

James rubbed his forehead and wondered what he'd done to become lumbered with this pair as friends since he'd moved to St Sebastian's. 'Look,' he said, slowly, 'there *isn't* a dog, and it *isn't* drinking vinegar.'

'But, Alexander said –' began Lenny.

'I know what Alexander said!' shouted James over the noise of classroom chatter. 'And if Alexander says one more word, it'll take him an awful long time to arrange his pencil collection from where I'm going to shove it!'

Lenny opened his mouth to ask whether the local dogs' home had been contacted to deal with the poor, vomiting canine when the door to the classroom burst open and Mr Watts lumbered in. Lenny scurried back to his seat.

'Who dragged *him* through a hedge?' muttered James, as he watched the teacher slam his briefcase on to the desk and fumble with the lock. He was rewarded with a kick on his own shin.

'Leave him alone,' ordered Alexander. 'It has often been said that care for one's appearance is inversely proportionate to one's IQ.'

Lenny turned to James for a translation.

'He means that he cares more about science than the way he dresses,' explained James. 'From the look of Mr Watts, he's just signed himself up as a contestant on a new game show called, *Whoops! Where's My Personal Hygiene?*'

Alexander swung his leg back again, ready to attack James's shin for a second time, but then he

stopped. He watched as Mr Watts gave up
fiddling with the lock, picked up his briefcase
and tried to bite it open. There was certainly
something different about the man, but he
couldn't put his finger on what it was.

It might have been the large flakes of ink-
stained skin that rained down from his face like
diseased dandruff, or the dull, faraway look in his
eyes. But what bothered Alexander most of all

was that the teacher no longer looked as though he had the mental ability to be teaching him his favourite subject.

'Still,' he grinned happily to James, as he pushed his chair back and stood up, 'it's nothing that can't be solved with another hilarious joke from the Alexander Tick humour database!'

James grabbed hold of his friend's sleeve and tried to pull him back into his seat, but it was too late.

'Mr Watts,' began Alexander, cheerfully, 'what did one magnet say to the other magnet?'

James folded his arms across the desk and buried his face in them, pretending he didn't know the headmaster's son.

Mr Watts, however, had stopped chewing at his briefcase and turned at the sound of his name, spitting out a gobful of leather. As he stared at Alexander, a glimmer of recognition flickered across his eyes, before dying out like the remains of a damp firework. The rest of the class, meanwhile, were busy tearing pages out of their exercise books to screw up and hurl at Alexander.

'Well,' said Alexander, as what had once been an English essay bounced off his nose, 'one magnet said to the other magnet, "I'm very attracted to you!"' He began to howl with laughter at the punchline. 'Attracted! Get it?'

As Alexander disappeared briefly beneath
a hail of paper balls, James glanced up at
Mr Watts, convinced that he must have lost
all patience with his star pupil by now. However,
the science teacher was just staring at Alexander
gormlessly, a trail of spittle slowly dribbling
from the corner of his mouth. James knew his
friend's jokes were bad, but they'd never had
that effect before.

'Oh, wait!' exclaimed Alexander. 'I've got
another one!'

James ducked as the hail of paper was replaced
by just about anything his classmates could find
to throw.

As first a CD case and then a stapler bounced
off Alexander, he beamed, 'Why did the lightning
hit the bus?'

I wish lightning would hit me, thought James,
as he waited for the headmaster's son to finish
the joke.

After a carefully calculated pause for effect, Alexander proclaimed, 'Because there was a conductor in it!'

Suddenly, Mr Watts laughed. Just a mixture of a grunt and giggle at first, but soon the giggle became a chuckle, and then the chuckle became a guffaw. Before long, the entire class was watching open-mouthed as their science teacher roared with laughter, hammering his fists on to his desk as tears rolled down his cheeks.

Alexander sat and folded his arms, a grin of triumph filling his face. 'There's a yellow highlight going on *that* one when I get home!' he announced, proudly.

CHAPTER 4
CURIOUSER AND CURIOUSER

'So, what do you reckon was the matter with Mr Watts?' asked James as he trapped the football beneath his foot before flicking it into the air, knocking it up with his knee and heading it over to Lenny.

'Who knows?' replied Lenny, the ball landing on his chest and dropping to his right foot, where he tapped it repeatedly into the air. 'He's a teacher; they're all weird.'

He passed the ball gently to Alexander who, in one smooth movement, swung out his leg,

missed the ball completely and crumpled to the ground, the contents of his school bag spilling out into the gutter. The boys always played football on their way home from school, and Alexander always ended up on his back.

'Were you born this geeky, or do you have to work at it?' asked James as he retrieved the football from underneath a parked car.

'Very funny!' retorted Alexander. 'Some of us were destined for greater purposes, such as science and history – not kicking a pig skin full of air around.' He stuffed a mountain of textbooks back into his bag and climbed to his feet. 'Which is why I'm worried about Mr Watts,' he continued. 'He's a scientist, but this afternoon his IQ appeared to be lower than a badger's bum.'

'There's definitely something wrong with him if he's laughing at your jokes,' said James, ducking as his friend threw a playful punch his way.

Lenny shrugged. 'Maybe his wife gave him a hard time this morning.'

Alexander shook his head. 'The man is, or should I say, *was* an intellectual giant. He doesn't have time for wives or girlfriends; science is his mistress!'

'You *what*?' mumbled Lenny, grabbing the ball and bouncing it as he walked.

'He means he's married to his job,' explained James. 'Plus, if he did have a wife, I doubt she'd let him leave the house each morning looking like he got dressed in the dark.'

Alexander sighed. 'When are you guys going to get it?' he moaned. 'Just because a chap doesn't follow the latest fashions doesn't mean he's an oddball!'

'Maybe not,' agreed James, 'but using the word "chap" in this day and age is a pretty sure sign of strangeness!'

Alexander ignored him. 'It still doesn't explain why he was acting so bizarrely this morning,' he said. 'At one stage, he froze completely for three minutes while writing on the board.'

'That's nothing,' said James. 'I asked him what the atomic weight of zinc was and he just groaned the word "Teach!" at me.'

'Well, he obviously wanted you to look the answer up for yourself,' claimed Alexander.

'You think so?' retorted James. 'And what did it mean when he tried to lick the pictures in my textbook?'

Alexander shuddered. 'I wondered why you had it laid out on the radiator all the way through French.'

'You don't think he's been poisoned, do you?' asked Lenny. 'He's always got a cup of tea in his hand, and there are a lot of chemicals in that classroom. Perhaps someone slipped . . . Oof!' Lenny hit the ground hard as a dark-haired girl appeared behind him and leapt on to his back. She reached down and tickled him hard.

'Leandra!' he yelled. 'Get off me, or I'll tell Mum it was you who broke her hairdryer!'

The girl jumped up. 'You wouldn't!' she cried, holding out a hand to help her younger brother to his feet. 'She thinks Dad fused it when he tried to wire his train set into the mains.'

Lenny wiped dirt from his school trousers.

'Anyway,' continued his sister, 'if you tell Mum about the hairdryer, I'll tell her that you've got a sick hedgehog hidden under your bed!'

James grinned at his friend. 'Are you still playing Super Vet?' he asked.

Lenny nodded. 'I found this one in the garden last week,' he explained. 'I think a cat had been at it, but it's making good progress.'

'I think it's really nice of you to care for sick animals,' proclaimed a voice.

The boys turned to find Leandra's best friend, Stacey Carmichael, standing behind them. The smile dropped from James's face.

'Oh, er . . . h-hello, Stacey,' he mumbled, blushing furiously.

The older girl flicked her curly blonde hair away from her face and fluttered her eyelashes at him.

'James!' she smiled. 'I didn't see you there!'

Alexander laughed at the thought of James being invisible to the girl of his dreams, but stopped quickly when the football bounced painfully off his face.

'So,' continued Stacey, plucking a loose thread from the hem of her ridiculously short school skirt, 'what were you boys talking about, other than hedgehogs?'

'We w–were, er . . . Th–that is . . . I m–mean . . .' stammered James, his cheeks climbing to a brand-new shade of pink. 'Mr Watts!'

'He was acting weird in science this morning,' explained Lenny, stepping in to try and help his friend.

Leandra snatched the football from James and spun it in her hands, nodding. 'You're telling us,' she exclaimed. 'We had a slide show with him this afternoon and Wayne Middlemiss had to operate the projector for him because he was trying to switch it on with his teeth!'

'And I swear his eyes were glowing red when the lights went off,' added Stacey.

38

'He's probably caught something,' announced Leandra, throwing the ball to Lenny. 'Let's hope it's nothing trivial!' She turned back to Stacey. 'Come on,' she said. 'Let's go and claim the telly before Super Vet here gets home and wants to watch nature programmes!'

The girls marched off, gossiping about the science teacher and how his now greenish skin tone had clashed with his maroon tie. The boys watched them leave.

'I guess it's not just us who noticed something odd about Mr Watts then,' said James.

Alexander took a step back and pretended to notice him for the first time. 'James!' he shouted, clasping his hands together and mimicking Stacey. 'I didn't see you there!'

Lenny snorted as he tried, unsuccessfully, to hold back a laugh.

'Stick,' said James to Alexander, 'how about we settle this the old-fashioned way?' He raised his fists and jumped around, laughing like a cartoon bad guy. 'Bare-knuckle boxing!'

'Now, now!' laughed Alexander, dropping his school bag and backing away. 'If you're not careful, James Simpson, I won't let you copy my science homework any more!'

As James chased his friend off down the street, Lenny wondered whether, given Mr Watts's current state of mind, there would be any science homework to copy out for some time to come.

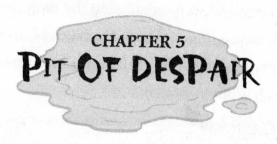

CHAPTER 5
PIT OF DESPAIR

Deep in the sewers beneath St Sebastian's School, William Scroggins splashed from one puddle to the next, utterly fed up. Eleven years old was the most boring age to be, he decided. He should know: he'd been stuck at eleven for the past six hundred years — ever since the day he'd died.

Entering the vast amphitheatre built by his fellow ghosts in the remains of their medieval plague pit under the school building, he gazed around, searching for something to do.

He spotted a rat snuffling up against the wall and picked up a twig from the nearest puddle. 'Fetch, boy!' he shouted, tossing the twig for the rat to chase. The rodent glanced up at him briefly with disinterest, then continued its search for food. William sighed.

A muffled bell rang out and a thousand pairs of children's feet hit the floor of the school at once. Pieces of old sewer pipe and, even worse, old sewer-pipe contents, rained down on William as the pupils thundered from one classroom to the next. He gazed upwards, longingly.

William would give anything to be a pupil at St Sebastian's. Even his treasured collection of items that had been flushed down the school toilets, that now included some ancient chewing gum, a pencil case and a shoe.

William had been up to the school on several occasions, but there was only so much fun you could have when you couldn't allow yourself to be seen by anyone.

By using a lot of energy, William *could* turn himself solid, but then he still looked like the small, undernourished farm hand who'd been claimed by the Black Death all those centuries ago. He'd spent a very uncomfortable afternoon being force-fed burgers and pies by a well-meaning dinner lady after trying that one out last spring.

There were three boys in particular who William wished he could be friends with. One was Alexander, a boy who – coincidentally – he almost looked the double of.

William didn't understand much of what Alexander said – a problem he shared with the majority of the school – but he always got the impression that the boy was clever. As William had been put to work on his parents' farm as soon as he could walk, being friends with a clever kid would be the next best thing to going to school himself.

Along with Alexander, there was the large boy, Lenny. He always smelt a bit funny but, from what William could gather as a result of eavesdropping on the boys' conversations in the toilets, this was because he rescued sick animals and nursed them back to health. Having spent the whole of his short life on the farm, William had a soft spot for anyone who was good with animals.

The third member of the group was James, who had only recently arrived at the school after his family moved into the area. James was definitely the leader of the trio, and the one who he hoped would one day agree to William's membership of the gang.

William sighed. Who was he trying to kid? St Sebastian's had been there for about a hundred years and he'd never been friends with any of the pupils. It wasn't going to happen now either. Not unless – for example – something incredibly *bad* happened and he had to save the school, and his favourite three boys, from total destruction.

'And then I transformed into a zombie and bit the science teacher!'

A familiar voice echoed along the sewer pipes, and William froze. There was only one ghost down in the pit who was wicked enough to bite a teacher and that was Edith Codd.

William edged his way out of the amphitheatre and into the tunnel often used by ghosts who wanted a bit of privacy. He walked as quietly as he could, listening hard for further details of Edith's latest plan to close down the school above them.

'You should see him now!' squealed the ghostly hag with delight. 'He looks like the result of one of his own bodged science experiments – and I can control everything he does!'

William peered cautiously round the corner to see Edith sitting underneath a dripping archway with his friend and one-time medieval leech merchant, Ambrose Harbottle.

'Watch this!' yelled Edith, jumping to her feet. She danced around the tunnel, slapping her own

face repeatedly. Hopping over to the rotting wall of the sewer, she rubbed her face up and down the mouldy bricks.

Ambrose stared at her open-mouthed, a partially sucked leech taking the opportunity to escape from his slackened jaws. Edith had really lost it this time!

'What you can't see,' explained Edith, wiping mould off her scabby lips, 'is that Mr Watts is copying my moves exactly in his classroom up above us!' She bent over and broke wind loudly. Muted howls of 'Oh, sir!', 'No!' and 'That *stinks*!' echoed down through the sewers, proving Edith's claims.

'I can make him do anything!' crowed Edith. 'Go on, Ambrose – make a request! Try me!'

Ambrose moaned. It was bad enough sitting and listening to Edith, but now she was expecting him to take part. 'Oh, I dunno . . .' he groaned.

'Come on!' coaxed Edith, skipping around the tunnel like a schoolgirl with a voucher for 'one free pony'. 'Just say something, and I'll force that ridiculous teacher to do it!'

'Don't want to . . .' mumbled Ambrose under his breath. He shuffled his feet through a puddle of what he hoped was runny mud and tried to avoid Edith's glare.

The female ghost thrust her hands on to her hips and shook her head. 'Right! I'll choose!' she announced. 'And as we're in the tunnel where boys bring their *ghoul*friends . . .' She leant in and kissed a very surprised Ambrose hard on the lips.

William stared in horror at the sight of Edith and Ambrose kissing. But his expression was nothing like those of the year-nine science class above as they watched Mr Watts snogging the science lab's resident plastic skeleton.

Edith pulled her lips away and smiled down at the terrified Ambrose. 'Well, if you think *that's*

good – just wait to see what else I can make that stupid, zombified teacher do!'

Ambrose held his breath, wishing for a little peace and quiet. Edith, meanwhile, struck a pose and started to rant.

'Using Mr Watts, I will destroy St Sebastian's and every wretched pupil and teacher within its disgusting walls! I shall not rest until the school is nothing more than a pile of rubble, and we tortured souls beneath it can finally get the peace and quiet we deserve!'

She smiled down again at Ambrose, who still hadn't quite recovered from his kiss. 'And, best of all, I won't even have to leave the sewers to do it!'

William listened in horror. He couldn't let this happen. He couldn't let Edith demolish the school in this way. And he certainly couldn't let her cause any harm to his friends up there. OK, they didn't know they were his friends, but he wasn't going to let a minor detail like that stop him.

Running as fast as he could, William raced for the pipes that led up to the toilets. He had to stop Mr Watts.

CHAPTER 6
THE PLAN

'I'm not sure I want to do this,' moaned
Alexander as he flicked through his science
textbook looking for something to teach himself.
Mr Watts had finally turned up to the class,
thirty minutes late, but was now busy sucking
the liquid out of a whiteboard marker.

'You haven't got to do anything,' responded
James. 'I'm the one who's going to search his
desk for clues as to why he's acting so strange;
I just need you to distract him.'

'How am I going to do that?' asked Alexander.

James stared at his friend, who had found a chapter about advanced chaos theory and was beginning to circle passages with a rainbow of coloured pens. 'I'm sure you'll find a way.'

'Hey,' said Lenny, as he perched himself on the edge of the desk. Aside from Alexander, none of the year-seven pupils was even attempting to do any work, and Lenny had finally become bored trying to coax a sparrow in from the windowsill. 'How long now?'

Alexander checked his watch. 'About three minutes,' he said. 'After which, we offer ourselves as a snack to the zombie that used to be Mr Watts.'

'For the last time, he's *not* a zombie!' moaned James. 'They don't exist!'

'I used to think so, too,' replied Alexander. 'But I've seen some pretty unusual things since I teamed up with you two, so I'm not ruling out the possibility that Mr Watts has become an unwilling servant of the undead.'

'This is different,' said James. 'Mr Watts is just ill.'

Lenny watched as the science teacher drained the contents of the marker pen and began to chew on a microscope. 'Yeah,' he said. 'I'm sure he'll be fine after a couple of painkillers and a nice lie down.'

The bell rang and the rest of the class leapt to their feet. 'Wait!' shouted Alexander, involuntarily. 'We haven't got our homework yet!'

Several of his fellow classmates pushed the headmaster's son hard in the back as they passed, the last sending him tumbling over a chair.

'Why did you let them do that?' asked Alexander from the floor.

'*Let* them?' retorted James, shaking his head. 'I don't know why you don't just paint a big target on your face, shouting out things like that!'

Lenny helped Alexander to his feet. The boys were now alone in the classroom with Mr Watts. It was time to make their move.

'Wait!' commanded Alexander as Lenny started to move towards the teacher's desk.

'What *now*?' hissed James.

'I'll tell him some more jokes to distract him,' explained Alexander. 'But I need my lucky showbiz medallion!' He thrust a hand into his pocket and pulled out what appeared to be a homemade necklace with comedy and tragedy masks sculpted from modelling clay on the end.

James stared at it. 'You've got to hand it to him,' he said to Lenny, 'the boy has no shame.'

Mr Watts had just picked up a freshly dissected frog and was lifting it towards his mouth when the grinning face of Alexander filled his vision.

'I say, I say, I say . . .' began the boy, causing the teacher to drop the dead frog in fright. 'What did the pupil say when the teacher asked him how many seconds were in a year?'

Mr Watts stared at him, unblinkingly.

'He said "twelve"!' finished Alexander. 'The second of January, the second of February, the second of March . . .'

The corners of the science teacher's mouth twitched. Alexander silently congratulated himself. *Got him!* he thought.

'Did you hear about the cross-eyed teacher?' he continued, grabbing a ruler and using it like a stand-up comedian's microphone. 'He couldn't control his pupils!'

Mr Watts's mouth twitched again, then broke into a shallow smile. 'Huh, huh!' he groaned.

'Then there's geography!' quipped Alexander. 'I mean, what do you call all those tiny rivers running into the Nile? Juveniles!'

That did it. Mr Watts burst into laughter again, slapping one hand hard on to his thigh and wiping tears from his vacant, red-rimmed eyes with the other.

As Lenny and James slipped underneath the teacher's desk, they heard Alexander launch into yet another dreadful joke: 'And in history . . . What did Caesar say to Cleopatra?'

With Mr Watts distracted, Lenny reached up and slid open the desk drawer. He felt gingerly about inside, grabbed the contents and pulled his haul beneath the desk to examine it. Fourteen identical red pens. 'No wonder hiding Mr Watts's pen never stops him from putting crosses all over my science homework!' exclaimed James.

'Er, guys . . .' called Alexander, as the teacher howled at yet another bad pun. 'I get the impression Mr Watts thinks this is a dinner date!'

'So?' whispered James. 'He can eat after you've finished entertaining him!'

'That wouldn't be so bad,' came the reply. 'Except he's looking at me as though I'm the main course! Hurry up!'

Lenny pulled his hand down from the drawer again. He was clutching an out-of-date flyer for a lecture on quantum physics at the local university. 'This is the only other thing in the drawer,' he said.

'In that case, we'll need to look in his briefcase. Can you reach it?' enquired James.

Lenny stretched out, his fingertips just short of the brown leather case. He shook his head. 'It's too far away. He'll see me,' he explained.

'Not if Alexander goes for the big finale,' said James. He quickly stuck his head up above the desk and winked to his nervous friend.

Alexander spotted the signal. 'Well, you've been a great audience,' he said. 'And I'd like to leave you with a selection of homework excuses . . . Like the kid who said he'd made a paper plane out of his, but it was hijacked!'

Mr Watts threw his head back and roared with laughter. Lenny spotted his opportunity and lunged forwards to grab the teacher's briefcase. He dragged it underneath the desk and handed it to James.

'It's locked,' he said to Lenny. 'What do you reckon the combination is?'

'I don't know,' the larger boy shrugged. 'Me and numbers don't mix. Especially the ones we're supposed to understand in this classroom.'

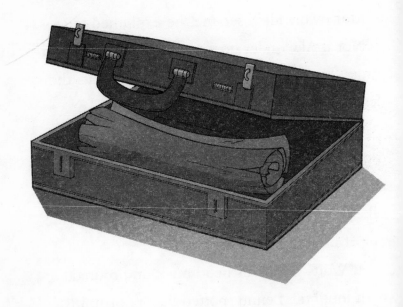

'The classroom! That could be it!' James twisted the numbers on the lock until they read 005 – the number on the door of the science lab. The lock opened with a soft 'click'. 'You're a genius,' he told Lenny.

While Lenny tried to work out exactly why he was a genius, James rummaged through the case and found the piece of evidence he was looking for.

Drawn on a sheet of paper, in shaky, spider-like handwriting, were some sort of chemical equations and plans. James swallowed hard as he read the heading at the top of the page: 'Operation Silent But Deadly – Killer Gas'.

CHAPTER 7
HOT AND SPICY

James and Alexander sat in silence, watching Lenny wolf down his third curry in a row.

'Hungry?' asked Alexander.

'Not really,' replied Lenny. 'I'm just trying to save myself from zombies.'

'That makes sense,' said James, unconvinced.

'I saw it in a film once,' continued Lenny through a mouthful of chicken korma. 'Zombies hate spicy food, so eating it keeps you safe.'

'Yep,' said Alexander. 'There's nothing the legions of hell like less than a touch of heartburn.'

'I don't mean zombies hate *eating* spicy food,' retorted Lenny. 'I mean if you eat it, it stops zombies from eating *you*!'

'You're making this up!' said James.

'I'm not,' said Lenny. 'I told you, it was in a film.'

'So you're saying that zombies are scared of curry?' asked Alexander.

Lenny nodded. 'It's like vampires and garlic.'

Alexander laughed. 'The only way curry is going to stop a zombie is if you eat enough of it to knock the monster out with your bottom burps!'

Lenny sighed, but carried on eating anyway. Just in case.

'Speaking of deadly gases,' began James, 'can we get back to Mr Watts's plan to destroy the school?'

'I still don't get it,' said Alexander. 'Mr Watts loves St Sebastian's. Why would he want to demolish it?'

61

Lenny shrugged, downing a bottle of water in one go to take the taste of the school curry away. 'Maybe he's heard so many of your jokes now that he's lost the will to live.'

'Ha, ha!' laughed Alexander, sarcastically. 'You weren't so critical of my comedy when I performed for him while you two hid under his desk.'

'It doesn't matter *why* he's doing it,' interrupted James. 'We know he's been transformed into some sort of zombie and that he's probably being controlled by someone – or something – else.' He unfolded the piece of paper he'd snatched from Mr Watts's briefcase and laid it on the table. 'I think we should be concentrating on *how*.'

Alexander scanned the list of chemicals on the paper. 'This is all stuff you can easily find in any school lab,' he explained.

'Can we get into the science store cupboard and remove them before he has a chance to mix them together?' asked Lenny.

62

'We could,' replied Alexander. 'But he'd only order more, and we can't be with him twenty-four hours a day. He'd make the gas sooner or later.'

'What does the gas *do* exactly?' asked James.

Alexander spun the piece of paper round to face him. 'Look at the ingredients, James,' he commanded. 'It's obvious what happens when you mix those particular components together!'

James stared at his friend. 'Let's pretend, for one moment, that I'm not like you,' he said. 'Let's pretend I don't spend all my spare time reading science textbooks and setting myself chemistry tests. Explain it to me like I'm a small child.'

Alexander shook his head. 'If you didn't waste every evening playing football, you'd know what this does when combined with this and this,' he said, pointing to various items on the list. 'The resulting vapour would knock out anyone who breathed it within a matter of minutes and, when the emergency services arrived and someone switched on an electric light, creating a spark . . . Boom!'

The boys sat in silence for a second, letting this latest information sink in.

'There has to be some way to stop him,' said Lenny. 'What do we know about zombies?'

'Zombies are like humans in many ways except that they lack conscious experience,' explained Alexander. 'They are known to eat the flesh of the living, and traditional methods of execution have no effect on them –'

'I've been meaning to ask you,' interrupted James. 'What *do* encyclopedias taste like?' He turned to Lenny. 'He means that zombies can't think for themselves, and you can't kill them.'

'You can scoff,' replied Alexander, 'but this information could save your life if, like I did, you find yourself faced with a ravenous creature of the night, armed only with a few weak puns.'

'For the last time, Mr Watts wasn't going to eat you!' cried James.

'So you say,' claimed Alexander. 'But you didn't see the hunger in his eyes. It was like Lenny at an all-you-can-eat buffet.'

'I've got no problem with pushing your face into this curry and holding you under until you stop wriggling,' said Lenny without looking up from his plate.

'Wait a minute,' said James. 'You said earlier that Mr Watts loves this school . . .'

'As much as any self-respecting teacher,' agreed Alexander.

'Well, is there a way we could turn him back to plain old Mr Watts?' asked James. 'That way he wouldn't go through with his plan.'

Alexander raised his eyebrows and stared at his friend. 'You're asking if there's a cure for being a zombie?'

James shrugged. 'I suppose so, yeah.'

Alexander giggled under his breath, shaking his head. The giggle became a cackle, and soon he was laughing as much as Mr Watts had in the science class. 'He wants to know if there's a cure for being a zombie!' he roared, pulling out a neatly ironed handkerchief embroidered with his initials and using it to wipe the tears from his eyes.

Lenny and James said nothing as Alexander's laughter gradually subsided and his fit of giggling ended with a long sigh.

'Well?' asked James again. 'Is there a way to cure him?'

Alexander shrugged. 'I don't know,' he admitted.

'We could try a stake,' suggested Lenny, shovelling more curry into his mouth.

'Do you ever stop thinking about food?' questioned Alexander.

'A wooden stake, not a beef steak!' insisted Lenny. 'Like you'd use with a vampire!'

'I doubt very much whether anything that has conventionally been suggested to work against vampires will have any effect on a zombie,' said Alexander. 'Plus, we're not killing Mr Watts by driving a wooden stake through his heart.' He looked from James and Lenny and back again. 'We are NOT killing him!'

James sighed. 'Then, short of following Lenny's example and drowning ourselves in curry, I don't know what to suggest,' he said.

'You don't want to do that,' replied Lenny, pushing his latest plate of brown sludge away. 'This stuff's disgusting.'

'We need more information,' suggested Alexander.

James nodded. 'I never thought I'd hear myself say this,' he said, 'but I think we should go to the library.'

CHAPTER 8
LOVE HURTS

'When you suggested coming to the library, I thought we'd be searching for answers in books,' said Alexander, as James logged into one of the three school computers connected to the Internet.

'You can spend hours flicking through dusty old pages if you want,' said James, 'but I think I'd rather just search for ways to combat zombies online. *Much* easier.'

'What are you going to do?' asked Alexander. 'Log on to www.howtostopazombie.com?'

There was a brief pause where nobody said anything before all three boys crowded together in front of the monitor as James typed the address in.

'I don't believe it . . .' said Lenny.

' "Everything you need to identify and stop zombies",' read Alexander aloud. 'Who sets up a web site like this?'

James shrugged. 'Someone who's had a similar problem to us,' he suggested.

'Well, let's reap the benefit of their experience,' said Alexander, as all three boys leant in and began to read.

William Scroggins squeezed himself between two bookshelves and strained to listen in on the boys' conversation. The gap was tiny, but he had managed to slide into it without too much trouble. Sometimes, being a ghost did have its advantages.

James, Lenny and Alexander were crowded around some sort of magic box. Pictures and squiggles, the meaning of which William could only guess at, flashed across the screen, but the trio seemed to understand them.

'It says here that zombies can be repelled by eating hot or spicy foods,' said James.

'I told you!' shouted Lenny, blushing when Ms Byron, the school librarian, glared at him and uttered a 'Shh!' that was loud enough to pierce glass.

Alexander opened a book and began to copy the squiggles down. 'Never a bad idea to take notes!' he announced to his friends.

William edged closer so he could eavesdrop some more.

'"Ways to identify a zombie",' read James, as he continued to scroll down the page. 'Get this down.' Alexander nodded, fountain pen poised above the pages of his notebook.

'"Zombies can be identified by their untidy appearance, poor personal hygiene and lack of reaction to everyday communication."'

'If that's the case, I reckon half the teaching staff are zombies!' exclaimed Lenny.

'There's more,' said James. '"Zombies have pale, rotting skin, no concept of their surroundings, and will do anything for a meal of human brains."'

'They eat brains?' asked Lenny. He glanced at James and then, slowly, both boys turned to stare at Alexander.

'What?' demanded their friend.

'If they eat brains, Lenny and I are mere snacks compared to you!' declared James. 'You must be every zombie's dream!'

'Don't be ridiculous!' sneered Alexander. 'Just because my brain is densely packed with facts and information doesn't mean that . . .' His voice trailed off and, after a moment's silence, he quietly added. 'Poo!'

'Don't worry!' said James. 'There'll be plenty of information on here telling us how to stop Mr Watts before he turns your brain into the dish of the day.' He clicked on another page and held his breath while it began to load.

William smiled. However the symbols on the magic box were talking to the boys, it was certainly giving them everything they needed to stop Edith from destroying the school.

He wished again that he was part of this group before an idea occurred to him. Concentrating hard, he turned himself completely invisible. Stepping out from between the bookshelves, he glanced around the room. The librarian behind the desk was looking his way, but obviously couldn't see him. This was his chance.

Striding over to the table with the three magic boxes on it, William settled into the small space between James and Alexander and sighed contentedly.

He was with his friends.

74

'Did you just hear something?' asked Lenny.

'No,' answered James. 'Like what?'

'I dunno,' replied Lenny. 'Like someone sighing.'

'It's probably just Mr Watts thinking about Alexander's brain,' said James.

'Will you two stop it?' demanded Alexander. 'My brain is no tastier than either of yours.'

James smiled. 'Yes, you just keep telling yourself that.'

'Shall I take over?' asked Alexander, removing the computer mouse from James's hand.

'No, I can manage,' responded James, snatching it back and using it to scroll down the page of ways to stop a zombie. 'It says here that we can destroy Mr Watts by decapitating him.'

Alexander turned to Lenny. 'That means chopping his head off,' he explained.

'Do you need me to tell you what *this* means?' Lenny asked, making a gesture with his fingers.

'We can also burn Mr Watts in a fire,' continued James, ignoring the look Lenny was now receiving from the headmaster's son.

'These are no good,' moaned Alexander. 'We're not out to kill the man, just to stop him from killing everyone else.' He leant in towards the screen. 'Are there any other suggestions?'

'There's a third page,' said James, clicking on the link.

The page loaded and all three boys began to read. They were silent for a moment, before Alexander finally spoke. 'How on earth are we supposed to do that?'

'I've no idea,' said James, 'but I'd say it's the only option left open to us.'

Wedged between them, William almost screamed with frustration. What had the boys discovered?

'D'you think it'll work?' asked Lenny.

'I can't see how it can,' replied Alexander.

'Neither can I,' agreed James.

Finally, William could take no more. 'What does it say?' he yelled.

'It reckons that –' began Alexander, before stopping suddenly and staring at James. 'Wow! You said that without moving your lips!' he exclaimed.

'Don't look at me,' replied James. 'I didn't say anything.'

Both boys faced Lenny.

'It wasn't me either!' he protested.

'Then who was it?' asked Alexander.

The trio paused for a second, then slowly turned in their seats to look at the only other person in the room: Ms Byron.

'I think she's listening in to our conversation,' said Alexander. Had he or the others been able to see William at that point, they would have noticed that he had his hand clamped firmly over his mouth.

'We'd better keep it down,' suggested James.

The boys pressed in together to stop the librarian catching a glimpse of the web page they were studying. William was squashed between them, but managed to stay silent.

'It claims that if a zombie finds love for a living person – and that love is returned – it will begin to return to normal,' said James.

'Well,' countered Alexander, 'they'll still technically be a zombie, but they won't decay any further, and any mind control that's taking place will be able to be broken.'

'But how do we get someone to fall in love with Mr Watts?' asked Lenny. 'I mean, it would be hard enough at the best of times, but the way he's looking and acting at the moment . . .'

'Are you suggesting that Mr Watts is unattractive to women?' demanded Alexander.

'Of course not,' responded Lenny. 'What woman wouldn't want a man who wears nylon ties and goes home every night smelling of sulphur?'

'However he smells, we have to make someone fall for him so we can save the school,' said James.

Unseen by the boys, William began to smile. He had a plan.

CHAPTER 9
GREY MATTER

'There is no way I'm going through with this!' insisted Alexander, as James and Lenny led him towards the science block.

'But I thought you'd jump at the chance to use your brain,' replied James.

'Yes, but not as bait!' insisted Alexander.

James pulled his friend aside as a group of year-eight pupils headed for the sports field. 'It'll take us ages to find Mr Watts a love interest, especially in his current state, so you'll have to distract him again while Lenny and I search for the gas.'

'I've told you,' said Alexander, 'if we take the gas, he'll only make more. We can't stop him.'

'Maybe not,' answered James, 'but we can stall him. If we take whatever gas he's already made, he'll have to start again. It'll buy us some time.'

'Plus, think of it as a chance to try out the latest jokes in your comedy database,' teased Lenny.

Alexander sighed. 'Sometimes I hate you guys,' he moaned.

'Hey! Stuart, Claire, Paul! How's it going, dudes?' enthused Alexander, as the year-ten science class began to stream out of the room.

James turned to Lenny and whispered. 'Dudes?'

Lenny shrugged. 'Maybe it's a science term . . .'

The three older pupils ignored Alexander completely and sauntered away, chatting amongst themselves.

'You know them?' asked James.

Alexander nodded. 'They're the founder members of the St Sebastian's after-school advanced chemistry club. I've been trying to get in with them for ages.'

'You're not a member?' said James, surprised.

'No,' replied Alexander, sadly. 'They say I'm too geeky. And they claim having the headmaster's son as a member would lose the group its street cred.'

Lenny started to choke on the chocolate bar he was eating.

James patted him on the back, helpfully. 'Well,' he said, 'save the school from a gas attack, and I reckon you'll be their new chairman.'

'You think they'll let me in?' asked Alexander, hope glinting in his eyes.

'Why not?' replied James. 'The hero who spotted a potentially deadly gas from a simple list of chemical ingredients? I wouldn't be surprised if they renamed the club in your honour.'

Alexander swelled with pride and pushed his way past Lenny. 'Excuse me,' he said. 'I have a science teacher to distract!'

As Alexander strode purposefully into the classroom, James turned to Lenny. 'Sometimes, it's just too easy,' he smiled.

Lenny and James entered the classroom to find Mr Watts fumbling with the lock on the store-cupboard door.

'He's trying to get the chemicals,' said James. 'We have to get him away from that cupboard.'

The boys nodded to Alexander, who took a deep breath and got to work.

'I say, I say, I say, sir – why does a flamingo lift up one leg?'

The teacher grunted and stopped his attempts to open the door in order to turn and stare at Alexander.

'Because if it lifted up both legs, it would fall down!' came the answer.

Mr Watts shook his head and returned to rattling the lock.

Alexander glanced briefly at James and Lenny, then tried again.

'I saw something out of bounds today,' he quipped. 'An exhausted kangaroo!'

This time, Mr Watts didn't even acknowledge that Alexander had spoken.

'It's not working,' Alexander said. 'He's not laughing at my jokes!'

'Maybe he *is* getting better after all,' suggested Lenny.

'He's becoming immune to your comedy,' said James. 'Like a virus becomes immune to its cure.' He thought for a moment, then announced: 'You have to show him your brain!'

'Show him my brain?' asked Alexander as the store-cupboard door creaked. The teacher was almost inside. 'What do you want me to do, crack my head open on a desk and tease him with the mushy bits?'

'Not your actual brain, you fool! Show him the size of your brain – how much you know!'

Alexander nodded and faced the zombie teacher once more. 'Absolute zero is the point where no more heat can be removed from a system, according to the thermodynamic temperature scale.'

Mr Watts looked up from the lock and turned a pair of interested eyes towards Alexander.

'Sodium has an atomic number of eleven, and can be found on the periodic table under the abbreviation, Na,' he continued.

The teacher took an uncertain step towards him. Alexander began to back away.

'There are two forms of electrochemical cells,' he said, moving further across the room as Mr Watts stumbled towards him. 'Spontaneous

reactions are present in galvanic cells, and non-spontaneous reactions in electrolytic cells.'

The zombie was groaning now, licking his lips as he advanced on Alexander, arms raised. James and Lenny watched, rooted to the spot, as their friend backed into a desk and was forced to climb over it to escape.

Mr Watts swatted the desk away and continued shuffling towards his star pupil.

'It's working!' shouted James. 'Keep going!'

'I don't like the look in his eyes!' yelled Alexander, overturning chairs as he retreated further across the room. They crunched under the science teacher's feet as he followed his prey.

James grabbed Lenny's arm. 'Come on!' he commanded.

The two boys raced for the store-cupboard door and examined it.

'There's no key,' said James. 'He's been trying to break in.'

'He was almost there,' agreed Lenny. 'The lock's nearly broken away.'

'Can you can finish the job?' asked James.

'I'll give it a go,' said Lenny grabbing hold of the door handle and pulling backwards as hard as he could. The wood around the lock began to crack and split.

87

'In nineteen thirteen, Henry Brearly discovered that adding chromium to low-carbon steel gave it a factor of stain resistance,' shouted Alexander. 'Although modern stainless steel may contain other elements, such as nickel, niobium and titanium!'

'Mmmm!' moaned Mr Watts, grabbing another desk and tossing it to one side, his eyes never leaving Alexander's head.

'He's eyeing up my brain, guys!'

'Almost . . . there!' groaned Lenny, sweat pouring from his face as he wedged a size-ten foot against the door and pulled the handle even harder. With a loud 'crack!', the handle and lock ripped away from the wood, allowing the door to swing open.

James spun round and shouted to Alexander, 'Keep Mr Watts busy!'

Alexander tipped over a table filled with experiments and leapt back as the teacher kicked it to one side effortlessly.

'I don't think that'll be a problem!' he replied. Staring into the zombie's eyes, he tapped the side of his head. 'You want what's in here, Mr Watts? You'll have to catch me first!'

'Why does that sound like a dare?' sighed James as he finally stepped inside the store cupboard.

CHAPTER 10
SEARCH AND DESTROY

'What exactly are we looking for?' shouted James from inside the store cupboard.

Alexander ducked as Mr Watts shot out an arm and tried to grab his hair. 'They'll be little black bottles with a skull and crossbones on!' he yelled in response.

James glanced up at Lenny, who was standing in the doorway to the cupboard. 'Is he serious?'

'Of *course* I'm not serious!' screamed Alexander, crawling underneath a row of desks as fast as he could. 'How should I know what you're looking for?' The zombie kicked one desk after another aside as he lumbered after the headmaster's son. 'Hurry up! I can't hold him off for much longer!'

James took a deep breath and began to search through box after box of science equipment, trying to find something suspicious even though he had no idea what it looked like.

William Scroggins froze as he watched the scene, concentrating hard on remaining invisible.

Alexander was on the floor, scuttling backwards as Mr Watts chased after him. James was overturning boxes inside a cupboard while Lenny was pulling shards of painted wood away from a broken door lock. His friends were in trouble.

What could he do to help? If he materialised in front of them, they might presume he was here to help the zombie, but there was very little he could do if he remained invisible. Or was there?

'Most babies are born with blue eyes because the protein melanin, which creates the brown pigment, needs to be darkened by exposure to ultraviolet light!' shouted Alexander, backing away before crashing into the whiteboard. He turned: a bench laden with Bunsen burners lay to his right, a metal filing cabinet to his left. There was nowhere to run without having to get past Mr Watts. Alexander's eyes widened with horror.

The zombie approached, saliva running down its rotting face, eyes fixed on the trembling boy with the plump, juicy brain.

The creature's fingers had just reached Alexander's face when a chair came crashing down on its head from behind. Mr Watts spun round, ready to lash out at whoever had struck him. But there was no one there.

Confused, the teacher turned back to Alexander and was about to grab hold of the boy once more when a desk flew across the room and crashed into the zombie, knocking him to the floor.

Alexander took the opportunity to escape and, using Mr Watts as a springboard, he leapt over the broken desk and scurried away as more items flew across the room, seemingly under their own power. *That's all we need*, he thought as a tray of beakers smashed against the zombie's back, *a poltergeist stirring things up!*

However, for the moment, the 'poltergeist' seemed to be on his side. As Mr Watts struggled to his feet, it ripped a cork noticeboard from the wall and flung it towards the roaring zombie.

'Well, if you can't beat 'em . . .' said Alexander to himself, hoisting up a portable TV the science teacher used for screening programmes of scientific interest and hurling it at the creature. Mr Watts took the full force of the TV on his chest and fell backwards, disappearing into a pile of broken science equipment.

'Whoever you are – thank you!' shouted Alexander over the din.

William smiled. Alexander had thanked him, but he didn't have time to savour the moment. Mr Watts was back on his feet and heading their way. Was there nothing that could stop that zombie?

Alexander had now pulled out the stationery drawer and was throwing individual pencils at the creature, pausing occasionally to slide the more collectable ones into his pocket.

Suddenly, the zombie howled. It was staring across the classroom at the store cupboard that James was still ransacking. Lenny, keeping watch, paled.

'J-James!' he stammered, 'it's seen what you're doing!'

The zombie began to stride towards the cupboard when a length of electrical cord suddenly whipped through the air and wrapped itself around the creature like a lasso.

Alexander caught on quickly and, grabbing a roll of metal wire normally used to demonstrate

sound waves, he began to run round Mr Watts,
helping to tie him up.

The zombie roared and stretched out its arms,
trying to break free, but the wire and cord just
pulled tighter, strapping the flailing limbs down
at Mr Watts's sides.

Inside the cupboard, Lenny was now helping James to search for any evidence of the gas. The boys pulled down entire shelves of scales, test tubes and glass dishes in a frenzy of activity. James glanced back and saw Alexander skipping around the growling zombie as though it was a rotting maypole. Shaking his head, James turned his attention back to the search.

William offered up a silent word of thanks to his father, who'd taught him how to rope a bucking horse on the farm all those centuries ago. He never thought he'd have to use that skill again, least of all against an out-of-control zombie.

He smiled as Alexander stood back from Mr Watts and grinned. 'Let's see you suck out my brains now!' he said, taunting the helpless monster. The zombie lurched forwards a few centimetres and Alexander jumped back, falling over a broken chair. Getting up, and assuring himself that Mr Watts was no longer a threat, he dashed into the store cupboard.

This is my chance! thought William and, focusing hard, he materialised in front of the zombie. Mr Watts gazed down at him, tilting his head to one side as he focused on the small boy.

'Yes, it's me – Alexander!' said William, trying to change his voice to impersonate the headmaster's son. 'Why don't you come and get me?' He edged backwards and the zombie followed, shuffling its legs as much as it could against the tight coils of wire and electrical cord.

'You want this great, big brain, don't you?' teased William. 'I know all sorts of things, like, er . . .' He scanned the room, looking for a subject he might be able to pretend he knew something about. His eyes fell on the broken TV. 'Like magic boxes! I know that's where the moving pictures live!'

Mr Watts paused for a second, unsure as to whether this could be the real Alexander. He didn't seem as bright as he had done previously. William sighed. Being Alexander was hard work.

'Guys! You'll never guess what's happened out there!' shouted Alexander as he bounded into the store cupboard. 'Things started to move by themselves, and I managed to tie Mr Watts up! Look!'

The boys stopped their search and poked their heads out of the cupboard door.

'Then where is he?' asked James.

Alexander dashed out of the cupboard and stared at the empty classroom in horror.

The zombie was gone.

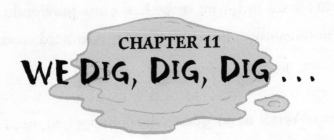

CHAPTER 11
WE DIG, DIG, DIG . . .

'Where can he be?' yelled Alexander, bending to search for the missing zombie under the desks.

'Where did you last see him?' asked James.

Alexander glared at him. 'He's a zombie, James, not a set of keys! He was right here, in the classroom!'

'Wherever he is,' muttered Lenny, 'you'll find him in the last place you look.'

'Of *course* he'll be in the last place I look!' roared Alexander. 'Because when I find him, I'll stop looking!'

Lenny's brow creased as he tried to work out the logic behind this.

'Well, we haven't got time to go searching for him now,' said James. 'We've got to find this deadly gas – if he's made any, that is.'

'Have you checked in those two boxes over there?' asked Alexander, pointing to the back of the store cupboard.

James shook his head. 'No, they're OK. They're marked "distilled water".'

Alexander sighed. 'You're incredible!' he cried. 'If the boxes said "aftershave" would you splash some all over yourself before speaking to Stacey?'

James blushed. 'You think that's the gas?'

Alexander grabbed a glass test tube from one of the boxes and held it up to the light, shaking it gently. Faint wisps of greenish vapour floated around inside, the only thing separating them from their victims being a little cork stopper.

'Bingo!' he replied.

The test tubes rattled as Lenny and Alexander carried a box each across the school car park, heading for the sports field.

'Be careful with those,' said Alexander. 'If the glass breaks, who knows what we'll release into the atmosphere!'

Lenny began to sweat. 'How deep will we need to bury them?' he asked.

'Not too far,' Alexander replied. 'Just deep enough so that they can't be broken by anybody walking over the grass above.'

'And you reckon underneath the goal on the football pitch is the safest place?' continued Lenny.

Alexander smiled. 'I may not be very sporty, but even I know there's only ever one goalkeeper there at a time!'

James dashed along school corridors, heading for the door that would lead him to the caretaker's room in the cellar. He kept an eye out for Mr Watts but, as none of the pupils he passed appeared to be either screaming or laughing, he figured the zombie teacher must be somewhere else by now.

As he reached the door to the cellar it was flung open, and Mr Wharpley, the school caretaker, thundered out. James tried to look as innocent as possible.

'Everything all right, Mr Wharpley?' he asked.

The caretaker waved a sink plunger in James's face. 'Why do you little monsters insist on using papier mâché?' he growled.

James could only shrug as the caretaker stomped off in the direction of the art room.

James watched him turn the corner and, when he was certain that the caretaker was safely out of the way, he pulled open the door to the cellar and darted through it.

Lenny scraped another handful of soil out of the hole with the gardening trowel and wiped the sweat from his face. 'You're certain you couldn't have found a decent-sized spade?'

'There wasn't one down there!' insisted James. 'I searched everywhere!'

'We'd be better off using our hands,' moaned Lenny. After a moment's silence, he glared up at James and Alexander. 'Well? Come on then!'

'Oh!' muttered Alexander.

The boys dropped to their knees and helped Lenny dig in the dirt.

'I still can't believe you convinced Ms Legg that you had to bury a time capsule as part of a science project,' said James. 'As PE teachers go, she's pretty hard to fool.'

'She wasn't too happy about abandoning the game,' explained Alexander, 'but I think she'd seen enough bad football for one afternoon and sent everyone in for an early shower.' He pulled his fingers out of the soil and examined his hands. 'It'll take me a week to get these clean again,' he groaned.

James ignored him. 'We still have to decide what to do about Mr Watts,' he said.

'I quite like him the way he is,' replied Lenny.

Alexander looked shocked. 'He wants to eat my brain!'

Lenny shrugged. 'Yeah, but we don't get half as much homework.'

'I'm not putting my education at risk just to give you less work to do!' exclaimed Alexander.

105

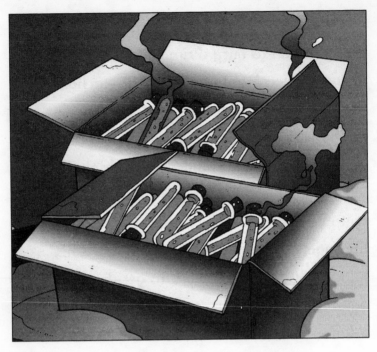

Lenny sighed. Alexander was off again.

'Well, maybe we could transform the rest of the teaching staff into creatures of the night . . .' he suggested. 'If Mr Hall was a vampire and Mr Parker became a werewolf, that would be our history and maths homework disposed of, too!'

'I was just saying!' mumbled Lenny under his breath.

'When you two have quite finished – I think the hole's deep enough now,' interrupted James.

Lenny nodded and carefully lowered first one, then the other box of glass test tubes into the hole.

'OK,' said Alexander. 'Now, we fill the hole slowly, so that the weight of the soil spreads evenly over the test tubes. We don't want any of them to break.'

Gently, the three boys began to scoop handfuls of dirt back over the boxes.

'Besides,' said Alexander after a moment's silence, 'I want my favourite teacher back!'

'Mr Watts is your favourite teacher?' asked James.

His friend nodded. 'His teaching methods may be a little coarse, and he might give out a lot of homework sometimes –' he said.

'*Might?*' muttered Lenny.

Alexander shot him a look. 'But he has such passion for his subject!' he continued. 'He loves

107

science and data. That's something you have to admire in a teacher, isn't it?'

'Is it too late to bury him as well?' James asked Lenny. The larger boy turned to hide his smile.

'You may mock, James Simpson,' jeered Alexander. 'But what will you do when you leave school if you haven't got a solid background in the sciences?'

James shrugged. 'Get an interesting and fun job?'

Alexander wiped his filthy hands along the legs of his school trousers. 'I don't know why I bother!' he grumbled.

'Oh, come on!' said James. 'I thought you'd like Mr Watts the way he is now. He laughs at your jokes; he certainly never did that before.'

'He never laughed at *anything* before,' added Lenny. 'It was like he'd had a sense of humour bypass.'

'I'm sure my comedy is strong enough to withstand the loss of one fan,' Alexander assured them, as he scraped the last of the soil over the hole and patted it flat with his hands.

'Are you sure?' enquired James. 'You take away one person who laughs at your jokes and that just leave you with –' he made a big show of counting on his fingers for a second, then pointed at Alexander – 'You!'

'I do *not* laugh at my own jokes!' said Alexander. 'I simply start the humour ball rolling.' And, with that, he stood up and strode off in the direction of the school.

James turned to Lenny. 'Start the humour ball rolling?' he asked as they climbed to their feet and started to follow their friend. 'I wonder what colour the sky is in his world?'

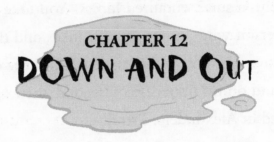

CHAPTER 12
DOWN AND OUT

'Will you hurry up?' demanded William as Mr Watts stopped to splash about happily in another puddle. Who would have thought the sewers had so much to offer in the way of entertainment?

'If Edith catches me with you, I'm in big trouble,' said William, as much to himself as the zombie. But any hopes of spurring the teacher forwards with this news were dashed at the sound of a small 'plop'.

'What was that?' William asked.

The zombie moved his shoulders in as close

a way as he could to shrugging, and bent down to fish about in the murky brown water. When he pulled his hand back out, he was holding an ear. His ear.

'Oh, no!' moaned William, looking at the red patch of skin on the side of the teacher's head where the ear had, until recently, been attached. 'You're starting to fall apart!'

William snatched the ear out of the zombie's hand just before he popped it into his mouth and started to chew. Realising he didn't have pockets, he sat it on a nearby pipe for safe keeping. 'We'll grab this on the way back,' he explained. 'Now, keep up and try to avoid losing any further body parts.'

William had taken two steps when he heard a low 'Uh-oh!' He turned to find Mr Watts sucking on one of his own severed fingers.

'This is going to be a long afternoon,' the ghost sighed.

111

Edith Codd skipped across the underground amphitheatre, flapping her arms about like a mad swan and making cow noises. 'Moo!' she yelled, reaching down to grab a lump of something brown and disgusting and rubbing it into her face.

She turned to Ambrose, who was viewing the insane display as he leant back against the upturned barrel Edith used as both her dressing table and ranting post. 'Something's not right!' she shouted, her face dripping with goo.

Ambrose watched as she stuck a finger up her nose and began to whistle loudly.

'You're telling me!' he replied.

As Edith continued to race around the cavern, dancing and imitating animals, Ambrose pulled a slim tin from a pouch slung around his waist. Opening it, he chose one of the six wriggling leeches inside and popped it into his mouth.

'Ah!' he sighed to himself, contentedly.
'A nineteen ninety-six. Good year!'

Edith arrived back in front of him and
Ambrose tried his hardest to look interested
in what she was doing.

'Mr Watts is no longer in my control!' she
yelled, spraying flecks of ectoplasmic spit
everywhere. 'No matter what I do, he's not
copying me!'

Ambrose was about to say that was probably
because, even as a disgusting zombie, Mr Watts
had his limits, but the thought was interrupted
by the sound of Edith screaming. She was
pointing to the entrance of the amphitheatre.
Ambrose followed her accusing finger and saw
William standing there, accompanied by the
zombified teacher.

'What the plague is he doing here?!' Edith
bellowed. 'No wonder I can't control him; the
spell only works when he's in the school!'

113

'I, er . . . I found him wandering the tunnels, Edith!' lied William. 'I think he might have stumbled down here accidentally, so I was taking him back up top.'

Edith closed in on William and circled him, slowly. 'Is that so?' she cooed, a little too calmly for the boy's liking. 'He just happened to find his way into the sewers?'

William nodded quickly. 'I guess so,' he said.

But Edith was on the scent. 'How do I know you didn't bring him down here to try and ruin my plans, eh?' she asked. 'How do I know that you don't want to keep the school open up there?'

'Don't be silly!' replied William, suddenly glad that he was almost transparent and unable to blush. 'I hate St Sebastian's as much as you do!'

'Oh, really?' said Edith, running bony fingers through William's mop of scruffy hair. 'It's just that you spend a lot of time up there. An awful lot of time.'

William swallowed hard. This was it. Edith had finally figured out that he was doing his best to keep the school open, and its pupils alive. There was nothing left to do but stand tall and take his punishment like a man.

'Where's his ear?' The voice rang out from the far side of the amphitheatre. Ambrose was striding over, staring at the side of the zombie's head.

'It's the spell!' cried Edith. 'Now he's down here I can't keep him in one piece!'

'That's why I was trying to get him back up to the school as quickly as I could,' said William, spotting a way out of the situation. 'His ear's on a pipe back down there, along with two fingers and three toes.'

'Three toes?' Edith squealed. 'What was he doing with his shoes and socks off?'

William closed his eyes to answer: 'Paddling.'

Several kilometres away along the sewer, a group of rats scattered at the sound of her scream.

115

'Get him back up there now!' Edith shrieked.
'Before we lose any more of him!'

Then the most unexpected thing happened.
Mr Watts spoke. 'The only thing I've lost is my
heart to you!' he oozed, winking at her.

The three ghosts froze.

'Who's controlling him?' demanded Edith. She
spun to face Ambrose. 'Is it you?'

The older ghost shook his head violently. 'I
wouldn't say anything like that to you!' he
admitted, honestly.

'Your teeth are like stars!' said the zombie,
reaching out and taking Edith's hand.

'Well, they do come out at night!' chuckled
Ambrose.

'Your lips are like petals!' added the teacher,
his eyes flashing.

'Bicycle pedals!' muttered William softly,
hoping that Edith wouldn't hear. But she was too
busy gaping at Mr Watts, open-mouthed.

The zombie continued. 'You have the body of an eighteen-year-old!'

'Well,' sniggered Ambrose, 'she'd better give it back before she ruins it!'

Edith's head snapped round to glare at him, and Ambrose paled even further than usual.

'Ignore them, my darling!' crooned Mr Watts, gently taking Edith's chin in his fingers and turning her face back to his. 'We don't need anyone but each other!'

Then, slowly, he leant in and kissed Edith full on the lips. When Ambrose had stopped vomiting and thought about it later, the mental image still made his toes curl.

Edith's hand slapped the zombie's cheek so hard that, for a moment, William thought they would have to add the teacher's head to the list of his missing body parts.

'How *dare* you?' screeched the hag. 'Get him back up to the school before I push his teeth so far down his throat he'll have to stick his toothbrush up his bum to clean them!'

William dragged Mr Watts across the amphitheatre, pausing only to pick up another finger that had dropped to the floor.

'Well,' he sighed to himself, 'that could have been worse!'

CHAPTER 13
IT MUST BE LOVE

'You're sure the ghosts are behind this?' asked Alexander, as the three boys picked their way nervously down the steps into the cellar.

'Think about it,' replied James. 'Who else would want to come up with a plan to destroy St Sebastian's?'

The faces of the school's pupils flashed across Lenny's mind. 'I can think of a few hundred,' he said.

The trio reached the caretaker's workroom in the cellar and found that the manhole that led down to the sewers had been opened, and the cover slid to one side.

'Mr Watts is down there,' said James.

'And you want us to join him?' moaned Alexander.

'You're the one who wants your favourite teacher back!' said James, pulling a small torch out of his pocket and angling the beam down the manhole. The dim light did little to break the blackness.

'I, er . . . I think Lenny should go first!' stammered Alexander.

'Why me?' asked Lenny.

'You're big!' answered the headmaster's son. 'If we come across the zombie, you might be needed to manhandle it!'

Lenny laughed. 'It's your brain he wants, Atomic Boy! I'm so bad at chemistry, I doubt there'll be enough in my head to make a small sandwich!'

Sighing heavily, Alexander pulled his handkerchief out of his pocket and gripped the top rung of the ladder with it as he began his climb down into the sewer. The last thing visible in the torchlight as his head disappeared were the embroidered initials: A.S.T.

'That last "T" should be an "S",' smirked James.

'This place could do with a good clean!' muttered Alexander, as the boys crept along the sewer tunnel which led underneath the school.

'I'll put it on "to do" list,' replied Lenny. 'Right under "Push Stick's face in that puddle of poo"!'

'Will you two pack it in!' hissed James. 'If the zombie *is* down here, I'd rather not announce our arrival too far in advance.'

'That's a thought,' said Alexander, stopping suddenly. 'What are we going to do with Mr Watts when we find him?'

'You don't know?' demanded Lenny. 'We're zombie hunting in the sewers and you don't know what we're going to do when we strike green?'

'Why should *I* be the one to think of everything?' asked Alexander, his face lit up eerily in the torchlight.

'Because you're the one who wants him back!' shouted Lenny. 'We were quite happy to let him sit motionless at the front of the class for the foreseeable future, remember?'

James sighed. 'We'll have to set a trap,' he said. 'We'll lure him into Mr Wharpley's workroom and cover him with a blanket or something. We just have to decided where to lie in wait.'

'Ear!' said Alexander.

James shook his head. 'No, I don't think here's very good. The ceiling's too low.'

'Not here – *ear*!' Alexander repeated, pointing at something at the side of the tunnel, his eyes wide with fright. James swung the torch around and the beam fell on the teacher's ear lying on the pipe.

'D-do you think it belongs to Mr Watts?' mumbled Lenny.

'I don't know,' responded James. 'Let's whisper sweet nothings into it and see if he comes for a cuddle.'

'How's he going to cope without an ear?' asked Lenny.

'He should be fine,' replied Alexander. 'The artist Vincent Van Gogh cut off one of his ears, and still continued to create some of the world's most wonderful paintings.'

'Yeah,' said James. 'But he couldn't wear his sunglasses again.'

'I think the ear is going to be the least of his worries,' said Alexander, grabbing the torch and shining the light further along the tunnel to illuminate two detached fingers.

'I think I'm going to throw up!' said Lenny.

'What's the matter?' asked Alexander. 'You're not scared are you?'

Lenny scowled at him. 'Of course not!' he insisted. 'It's all that curry I had for lunch repeating on me.'

'I thought I could smell something horrible,' said Alexander.

Lenny stared, unblinkingly. 'You're standing in a pool of human waste and you're blaming me for the smell?' he asked.

'Shhh!' commanded James. 'Someone's coming!' He grabbed the torch back and swung the beam of light along the tunnel in the direction of the shuffling noise.

At first, the boys couldn't make out anything in the darkness but, after a moment, the stumbling figure of Mr Watts appeared, most of his detached fingers and toes clumsily glued back on with sewer sludge.

'He's come for my brain!' squealed Alexander, pulling his school jumper up over his head as though knitwear was the world's most powerful zombie repellent.

'There's someone with him!' shouted Lenny but, as James whipped the torch around to look, the smaller figure disappeared, almost into thin air.

Alexander was trembling now. 'Take the part of my brain that speaks foreign languages,' he whimpered. 'Just leave me the science, the history and the ability to tell jokes!'

James watched, rooted to the spot as Mr Watts lumbered up to Alexander . . . and passed him by, pausing only to snatch his missing ear and fingers from Lenny's hand and stick them in place with goo from the sewer walls.

'Where's he going?' asked Lenny.

'Only one way to find out,' said James and, grabbing Alexander's arm, he began to follow the staggering zombie.

By the time the boys had climbed the ladder back into the caretaker's room, Mr Wharpley was in there, yelling at the zombie teacher and demanding to know what was going on.

Pushing him to one side and sending the caretaker crashing into a shelving unit, Mr Watts began to climb the stairs.

'He's going for the gas!' said James.

'Does he know what we've done with it?' asked Lenny.

'Even if he doesn't, he's strong enough to start tearing the school apart by hand,' answered James. 'We'll have to follow him.'

Alexander pulled his jumper down and began to feel around his head. 'Which bit did he take?' he said. 'Can I still learn maths?'

'There won't be anywhere *to* learn maths if we don't stop him,' yelled James and began to dash up the stairs. Suddenly, there was a piercing scream from the corridor above them. 'Quick! He's started!'

The three boys bounded up the metal steps and through the door, then stopped. Mr Watts had apparently blundered through the door and straight into Miss Keys, sending her sprawling to the floor.

The zombie bent over her. Alexander turned away, unable to watch the moment that Mr Watts cracked open the school secretary's skull and began feasting on the contents. But the teacher simply helped Miss Keys to her feet.

'I'm terribly sorry,' he said smoothly.

'That's quite OK,' replied Miss Keys, staring deep into the zombie's eyes. 'I wasn't watching where I was going!'

'Allow me to assist you back to your office,' said Mr Watts, the green tint in his skin starting to fade.

The boys watched, amazed, as the teacher's glowing eyes dimmed and the body parts glued on with sludge quickly fused into place.

By the time Mr Wharpley burst out of the door behind them, Mr Watts looked almost human again.

'What time do you finish work today?' asked the teacher, as he wrapped an arm around Miss Keys's shoulders and led her away. She was blushing deeply.

'So, do you think he's cured?' asked Lenny.

'Let's find out,' replied James, smiling at Alexander. 'Do your stuff!'

Alexander grinned and shouted down the corridor: 'Hey, sir!' Mr Watts stopped and turned back. 'What do vampires have at eleven o'clock every day?' After waiting his tried-and-tested optimum pause time, Alexander grinned. 'A coffin break!'

Mr Watts shook his head and, without so much as a smile, turned his attentions back to the school secretary.

'Well, I'll be adding this to my file of baffling events!' announced Alexander as he watched Mr Watts walk away.

James and Lenny exchanged a glance.

'You don't *really* have a file like that, do you?' asked James.

Alexander nodded. 'It's in the top drawer of my bedroom filing cabinet!'

Lenny grinned. 'If it's full of things he finds baffling, it must be HUGE!'

As the boys wandered towards the exit, laughing, Mr Wharpley closed and locked the door to the cellar. Had it remained open, he would have heard a scream echoing out from the sewers below.

'You haven't seen the last of me, St Sebastian's!' wailed a shrill, female voice. 'Mark my words!'

SURNAME: Tick

FIRST NAME: Alexander
(sometimes known as 'Stick' cos he's so small and skinny)

AGE: 11

HEIGHT: 1.3 metres

EYES: Blue

HAIR: Blonde

LIKES: School (especially science and history lessons), homework, collecting gags for his jokes database, sharing his vast knowledge with others

DISLIKES: Having his head flushed down the toilet by Gordon 'The Gorilla' Carver; being yelled at by his father, Mr Tick; being a bit small for his age

SPECIAL SKILL: Storing endless facts in his huge cranium, especially anything to do with science or history

INTERESTING FACT: Alexander's middle name begins with 'S' but he refuses to tell anyone what it stands for - it's bound to be something embarrassing if Mr Tick had anything to do with choosing it . . .

For more facts on Alexander Tick, go to **www.too-ghoul.com**

Alexander Tick's
Joke File
(page 1,548)

Q Why did the orange stop?
A Because it ran out of juice!

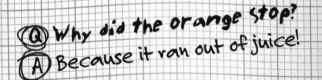

Q What word is always pronounced wrong?
A Wrong!

Q What do sea monsters eat?
A Fish and ships!

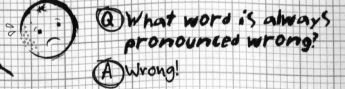

Q What do you give an injured lemon?
A Lemon-aid!

NOTE TO SELF: input these into jokes database at earliest convenience

Q Why did the chewing gum cross the road?

A It was stuck to the chicken's foot!

Q Why did the jelly wobble?

A Because it saw the milk shake!

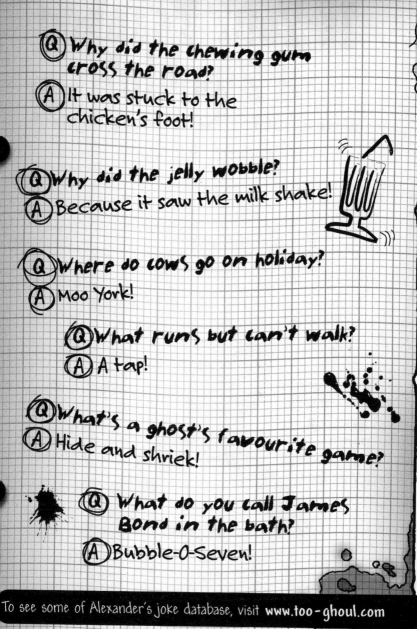

Q Where do cows go on holiday?

A Moo York!

Q What runs but can't walk?

A A tap!

Q What's a ghost's favourite game?

A Hide and shriek!

Q What do you call James Bond in the bath?

A Bubble-O-Seven!

Is Your Teacher a Zombie?

Watch out for the tell-tale signs!*

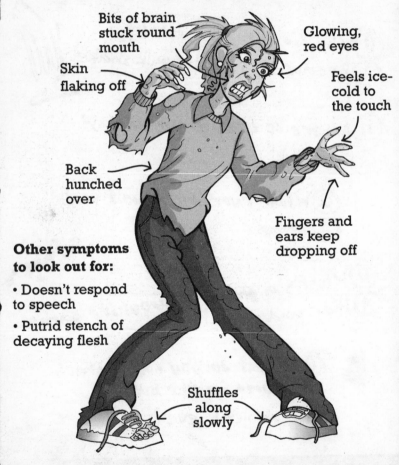

Bits of brain stuck round mouth

Glowing, red eyes

Skin flaking off

Feels ice-cold to the touch

Back hunched over

Fingers and ears keep dropping off

Other symptoms to look out for:

• Doesn't respond to speech

• Putrid stench of decaying flesh

Shuffles along slowly

*Please note: some teachers may exhibit all of these signs without actually being zombies. Especially with science teachers, it can be difficult to tell. If in doubt, steer clear and keep your brain well covered.

What Makes Alexander Tick?

Here's what goes on in the big brain that
Mr Watts wanted for his zombie dinner!

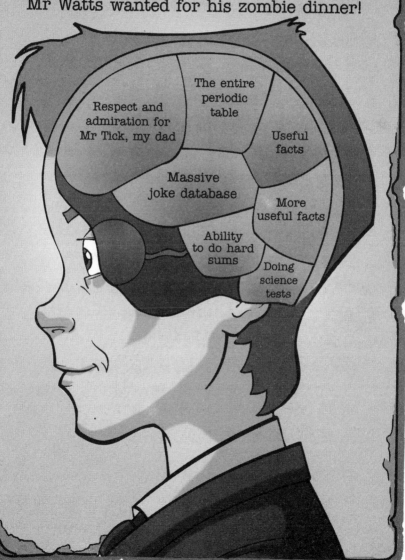

Zombie Facts

- Zombies are the undead — corpses that are brought to life to terrorise the living!

- One bite from a zombie can turn you into one of their deadly army.

- Zombies don't eat normal food. They feast on human brains whenever they feel peckish!

- Zombies can only think about their next meal and wiping out any humans they happen to meet.

- There is no cure for being a zombie. But a victim of zombification can be brought halfway back to normal if they fall in love with a non-zombie.

- Zombies are constantly decomposing every day, so bits of them drop off and they smell of rotting flesh.

- If you see a zombie walking round your school, don't panic. It could just be a particularly ugly year eleven going to a maths lesson.

- If you're sure there's a zombie on the loose, run for your life — and cover your head with a crash helmet!

Can't wait for the next book in the series?
Here's a sneak preview of

THE IN-SPECTRES CALL

available now from all good bookshops,
or **www.too-ghoul.com**

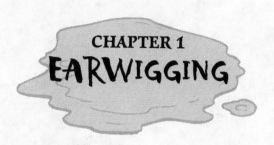

CHAPTER 1
EARWIGGING

'What's that droning noise?' grumbled Edith Codd, leader of the plague-pit ghosts. She frowned and glared about the cavernous amphitheatre that had been built over the centuries in the sewers deep under St Sebastian's School.

Ambrose Harbottle, a leech merchant before the Black Death had carried him off over six hundred years earlier, was leaning against a stone pillar. He was humming a happy little ditty about 'juicy little leeches' to himself as he sorted through a tin of them. He popped one

139

in his mouth and chewed noisily, like a dog gnawing gristle.

'Shhh!' Edith hissed, scowling. '*Listen!*'

A loud voice was carrying down the pipes from the school above. 'It's that horrible headmaster,' she said. 'He thinks he's so incredibly important!'

'He's not the only one . . .' Ambrose whispered to William Scroggins, a young ghost who sat at his feet. William choked back a giggle.

'He's such a bore! I can't think *why* he imagines anyone wants to listen to him . . .' Edith went on, shaking her head.

Ambrose nudged William and smirked. William spluttered.

'He's so full of his own importance – he's like a puffed-up town crier!' grumbled Edith.

'Takes one to know one,' Ambrose muttered. William sniggered.

'It's bad enough having to put up with those horrible children laughing and shouting all day,' moaned Edith. William smiled wistfully at the thought of the fun the pupils were having, 'without that idiot droning on and on!'

She stopped suddenly, frozen in place like a stoat scenting a particularly delicious rabbit. Her large nostrils flared and her eyes narrowed.

'What was that . . .? A visit from the *who* . . .?'
she hissed. She pressed her ear up against the
rusty pipe.

A small spider gasped, screwed up its face, spat
and ran away as a waft of Edith's breath hit it.

Up in the school, high above the ghosts, Mr Tick
the headmaster was in St Sebastian's staffroom,
trying hard to get the attention of the assembled
teachers. They lay slumped in their chairs,
sipping coffee.

'Listen, everybody!' Mr Tick demanded,
clapping his hands. 'We are having a visit from
the school inspectors this afternoon. There is, of
course, nothing for *most* of us to worry about.
May I remind you that the inspectors will be
listing the strengths and weaknesses of the school
during their visit. The last time they came, they
noted a lack of care and guidance from some of

the teaching staff. Can't possibly see how they got that idea, ha, ha! I will, of course, be showing them round all the new facilities personally, and Miss Keys shall serve them tea in my beautifully decorated office –'

'Won't they want to talk to the children, too?' asked Ms Legg, the PE teacher.

'Why on *earth* would they want to do th–
I mean, no, I shouldn't think so – busy people
and all that . . .'

Edith pressed her ear against the pipe. 'A visit
from the In-Spectres? That sounds interesting . . .'
whispered Edith to herself. 'It sounds very
official . . .'

'I remember the last report,' Mr Watts, the
science teacher, grumbled. 'I seem to recall that
school leadership and management weren't seen
as too hot either –'

'I don't remember any such thing,' harrumphed
Mr Tick. 'You must have misread the report . . .
Anyway – right! That's settled then. Everyone must
be on the look-out for visitors with clipboards. I
shall be accompanying them round, of course . . .'

Edith could *hear* the man smiling, his voice was
so smarmy.

'We always know when there are visitors in
school,' female voice said quietly. Edith strained

to hear. 'We actually get to *see* the headmaster in the classrooms for once . . .'

Edith jumped backwards as a hoot of laughter that suddenly changed to a coughing fit rumbled down the pipes.

'I heard that!' the headmaster growled. 'Look – the bottom line is this: we must all pull together to convince the inspectors that we have a smooth-running school filled with caring teachers and happy pupils, or St Sebastian's will close. I don't think anybody here wants to be out of a job, do they?' Edith could hear rustling, as though people were shuffling about in their seats. 'No. Funny that – I didn't think so. There aren't too many jobs in Grimesford, unless you count the glue factory, and I don't think they're hiring. So it's up to you lot.'

Edith heard heavy footsteps as someone stalked out of the room. She heard the doors swish and then a murmuring as people started to talk.

'Well, I'm not looking forward to it, I must say! Those people breathing down your neck. What do they know about life in the raw, at the chalkface . . .?'

'At least it'll keep old Tricky Ticky on his toes!' a voice laughed.

'I get nervous when I'm being watched . . . I set fire to my tie in the lab by accident last time . . .'

Edith jumped up, hugging herself with excitement.

'This is great news!' she giggled. The words sounded wrong coming from Edith's thin lips. William shuddered. 'These In-Spectres have got the teachers and that horrid headmaster rattled, so they *must* be a good thing! There was me thinking the man was totally useless, then he comes up with something that could sink St Sebastian's for good! Oh, happy days!'